Cinderella

سندريلا

English - Arabic

THE URBANA FREE LIBRARY

W9-BCD-361

TALES & FABLES

Excellence in Children Books

DISCARDED BY THE URBANA FREE LIBRARY

The Urbana Free Library
To renew: call 217-367-4057
or go to urbanafreelibrary.org
and select My Account

Once upon a time there was a beautiful girl named Cinderella. Her father died when she was very young and her life became lonely and sad.

After her father's death, she was left in the care of her step-mother who had two daughters of her own.

كانت في قـديم الزمان، فتاة جميلة اسـمها ســندريلا، وتوفى أبوها حين كانت صغيرة جدا، فأصحبت حياتها حزينة وكانت تشعر بالوحدة.

وبـاتت في رعاية زوجة أبيها بـعد وفاته وكانت لزوجة أبيها بنتان.

Cinderella's step-mother and two step-sisters were very ugly and cruel. They forced Cinderella to do all the house work. They gave her only rags to wear and left-over food to eat.

وكانت زوجة أبيها وبنتاها قبيحات وقاسيات جدا، وكن يجبرن سندريلا على أن تعمل كل الأعمال المنزلية، وكن يعطينها خرقا بالية لترتديها والفضلة من الطعام للأكل.

One day, Cinderella's step-mother said, "We are going to the palace. The charming Prince is having a royal ball to find himself a bride. I hope he will marry one of my daughters. But Cinderella, you must stay at home and wash all the dirty clothes and dishes."

وقالت زوجة أبيها يوما، "نحن نذهب إلى القصر. ويعقد الأمير الجميل الفاتن حفلة راقصة ليختار بها عروسا لنفسه. وأنا آمل أنه سيتزوج إحدى بناتي. و يا سندريلا عليك أن تمكثي في المنزل وتغسلي الملابس الوسخة والصحون."

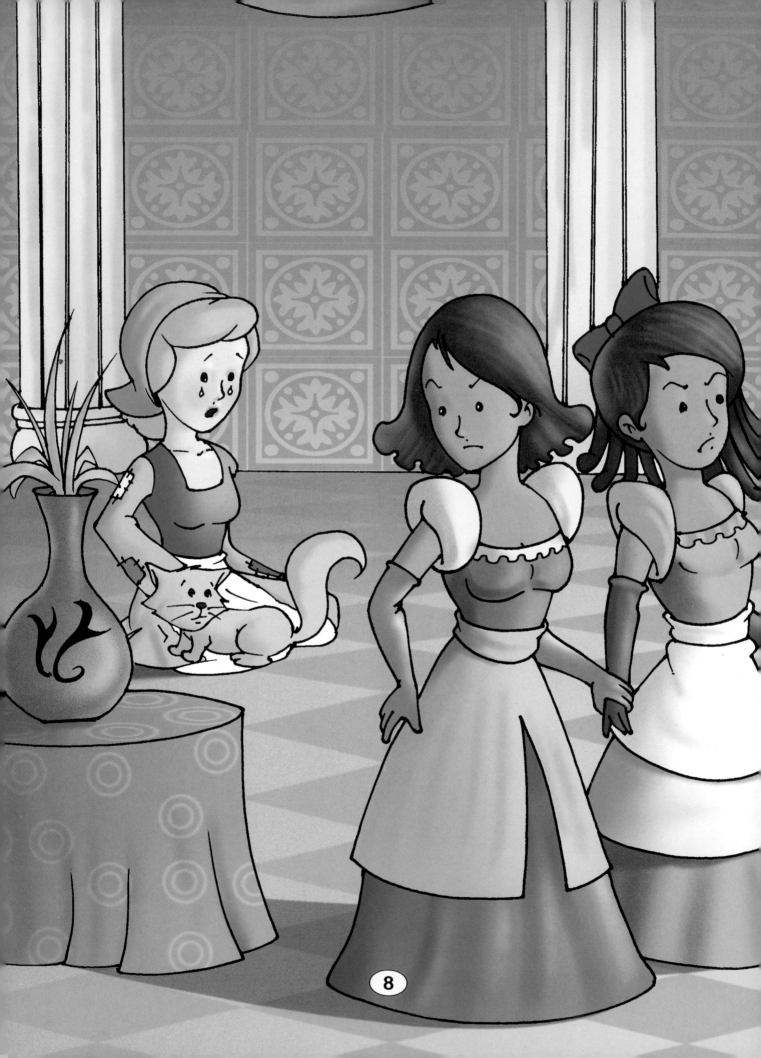

8

Cinderella felt very sad as she saw her two step-sisters wearing lovely clothes and going off to the ball. She sat down with her pet cat, and began to cry.

"I wish I could also go to the ball and meet the Prince," she whispered to her cat.

شعرت سندريلا بيأس شديد، حين نظرت بنتي زوجة أبيها تلبسان الملابس الجميلة، وتخرجان إلى الحفلة فجلست مع قطتها الأليفة، وبدأت تبكي.

وهمست إليها "أنا أتمنّى أن أذهب إلى الحفلة وأن أقابل الأمير."

Suddenly, a kind-hearted fairy appeared before Cinderella. "Don't be sad, Cinderella," said the fairy.

فجأة، ظهرت لها جنية رقيقة القلب، وقالت "لا تحزني يا سندريلا."

"Who are you?" Cinderella asked.

"I am your fairy godmother and I will make your wish come true! Fetch me a large pumpkin," said the fairy. Then she turned to Cinderella's cat and said, "Run along and fetch me four mice."

وسألتها سندريلا "من أنت؟"

"أنا عرّابــتك الجنية وأنا أحقّق أمنيتك! اجلبــي يقــطينا كبيرا،" قـالت الجنية. وبـعد ذلك اتجهت إلى قطة سـندريلا، وقالت، "انصرفي، واجلبي أربع فأرات".

Cinderella and her cat did as they were told. The fairy waved her magic wand over the pumpkin and turned it into a magnificent golden coach. Then she turned the four mice into horses and the cat into a well-dressed coachman.

وعملت سندريلا وقطتها كما قيل لهما. وحركت الجنية عصاها السحرية فوق اليقطين، وحولته إلى مركب ذهبي ممتاز. ثم قلبت الفأرات الأربع أفراسا، كما قلبت القطة سائق المركب في زي جميل.

"But fairy godmother, I can't go to the ball in these rags!" Cinderella said. The fairy smiled and waved her magic wand over the poor girl. Cinderella's rags changed into a beautiful dress. Her torn shoes turned into dainty glass slippers.

وقـــالت ســـندريلا، "ولكن أيتها العرابـــة الجنية، أنا لا أستطيع أن أذهب إلى الحفلة في الملابـس البالية" فابتسمت الجنية وحركت عصاها السحرية على الفتاة الفقيرة، وغيرت ملابسها البالية إلى ملابـس أنيقـة كماغيرت أحذيتهاالممزّقـة إلى نعال زجاجية جميلة.

"Now go to the ball Cinderella. But remember to return before midnight because at the stroke of twelve my spell will end and everything will turn back to what it was!"

Cinderella happily climbed into her golden coach and rode off to the palace.

"اذهبــي الآن إلى الحــفلة ولكن عليك أن سندريلا ! ترجعي قبـل منتصف الليل، فسـينتهي سحـري إلى السـاعة الثانية عشرة، وسيتحول كل شئ إلى ما كان!"

صعدت سندريلا مركبا ذهبيا بفرح، وتوجهت إلى القصر.

When Cinderella entered the palace, everybody turned and stared at her. They had never seen anybody so beautiful. Cinderella's step-mother and step-sisters did not recognize her in her gorgeous dress and dainty glass slippers. They stared at her with envy.

وعندما دخلت سندريلا القصر، استدار كل شخص إليها، وجعلوا يحدقون إليها، إنهم لم يروا أبدا أي شخص أجمل منها قط، ولم تعرفها زوجة أبيها ولا بنتاها في ملابس فاخرة وشباشب زجاجية جميلة، ونظروا إليها بنظرات حاسدة.

The Prince fell in love with beautiful Cinderella the moment he saw her. He danced with Cinderella the whole night. Cinderella felt so happy that she forgot all about her fairy godmother's magic spell.

When the clock began to strike the hour of midnight, she suddenly remembered her fairy godmother's warning. Cinderella quickly ran out of the palace.

ولما نظر الأمير إلي سندريلا الجميلة وقع في حبها، ورقص معها طول الليل وفرحت سندريلا كثيرا حتى نسيت كل شيئ عن سحر العرابة الجنية.

وحينما كادت الساعة أن تدق نصف الليل، تذكرت سندريلا فجأة تحذير العرابة الجنية، وجرت سريعا إلى خارج القصر.

As she ran down the stairs, one of her glass slippers came off. But she did not stop, and left before the spell ended.

The Prince chased her but he could not find her. Then he saw her glass slipper lying on the palace stairs. He sent his ministers to search the whole kingdom and try the slipper on every girl until Cinderella was found.

ولما نزلت سندريلا من السلّم خرج أحد شباشبها الزجاجية ولكنها لم تتوقف وتركت المكان قبل أن ينتهى السحر.

وتعقبها الأمير ولكنه لم يجدها، ثم رأى شبشب الزجاج مهجورا على سلّم القصر، فأرسل وزرائه في البحث عنها في جميع أنحاء المملكة، وأن يجرّبوا الشبشب على كل فتاة حتى يعثروا على سندريلا.

A few days later, the ministers came to Cinderella's home. Cinderella's step-sisters tried to fit into the glass slipper but their feet were too big.

"May I try it too?" Cinderella asked shyly. Cinderella knew the slipper would fit just right.

وبــعد بــضعة أيام جاء الوزراء إلى منزل ســندريلا، وحــاولت بــنتا زوجة أبـــيها أن يوافق الشبشب الزجاجي أقدامهما، ولكن أقدامهما كانت كبيرة جدا.

"هل لي أن أحاول ذلك أيضا" طلبت سندريلا باستحياء، وكانت تعرف أن الشبشب سيوافق قدمها.

Cinderella put on the dainty glass slipper. Magically, her old worn clothes turned into the beautiful dress from the royal ball.

Cinderella's step-mother and step-sisters gasped with envy and surprise. They could not believe Cinderella was the beautiful girl from the ball.

The ministers said, "Come with us, Cinderella! The Prince is waiting for you."

وضعت سندريلا قدمها في الشبشـب الزجاجي الناعم. فتحولت ملابسها البالية سحريا إلى الملابس الأنيقة من الحفلة الملكية.

تلهّفت زوجة أبيها وبنتاها حقدا ودهشة، ولم يستطعن أن يصدقن بأن سندريلا هي الفتاة الجميلة من الحفلة.

قـال الوزراء، "تعالي معنا يا سندريلا! والأمير هو في انتظارك."

Cinderella thanked her kind-hearted fairy godmother who had made her wish come true.

The Prince married Cinderella and they lived happily ever after.

وشكرت سندريلا لعرابتها الجنية الرقيقة القلب التي حققت أملها.

تزوج الأمير سندريلا وعاشا بسعادة دائمة.